THE FALLING RAINDROP

by

Neil Johnson & Joel Chin

TRICYCLE PRESS
Berkeley

Clouds are made of water vapor. When clouds get heavy, the water vapor falls as rain
onto the warm earth. The warmth turns rain into steam. As the steam rises,
it cools, becomes water vapor, and becomes part of a cloud again.

Published in the United States by Tricycle Press, an imprint of the Crown Publishing Group,
a division of Random House, Inc., New York.
www.crownpublishing.com
www.tricyclepress.com

Tricycle Press and the Tricycle Press colophon are registered trademarks of Random House, Inc.

Library of Congress Cataloging-in-Publication Data
Johnson, Neil, 1963-
  The falling raindrop / by Neil Johnson and Joel Chin. – 1st ed.
     p. cm.
  Summary: A newborn raindrop falls happily from the sky, until he begins to worry about what
might happen next.
  [1. Raindrops–Fiction. 2. Rain and rainfall–Fiction. 3. Worry–Fiction.]
I. Chin, Joel, 1968- II. Title.
  PZ7.J63419Fal 2010
  [E]–dc22
                        2009016779

ISBN 978-1-58246-312-4 (hardcover) — 978-1-58246-344-5 (Gibraltar Library Binding)

Printed in Malaysia

Design by Colleen Cain, based on the authors' original design
The text of this book is set in Simoncini Garamond.
The art was created digitally.

1 2 3 4 5 6 —15 14 13 12 11 10

First Edition

For Ryan and Lara

It was a stormy day.

Dark clouds gathered.

The wind howled.

Lightning flashed.

And thunder boomed.

As the storm rumbled and shook, something wonderful happened in the clouds: a raindrop was born.

With a little gasp and a big smile,
the raindrop began to fall.
"I'm alive!" he shouted.

He felt like he was flying
as he whizzed down
through the clouds.

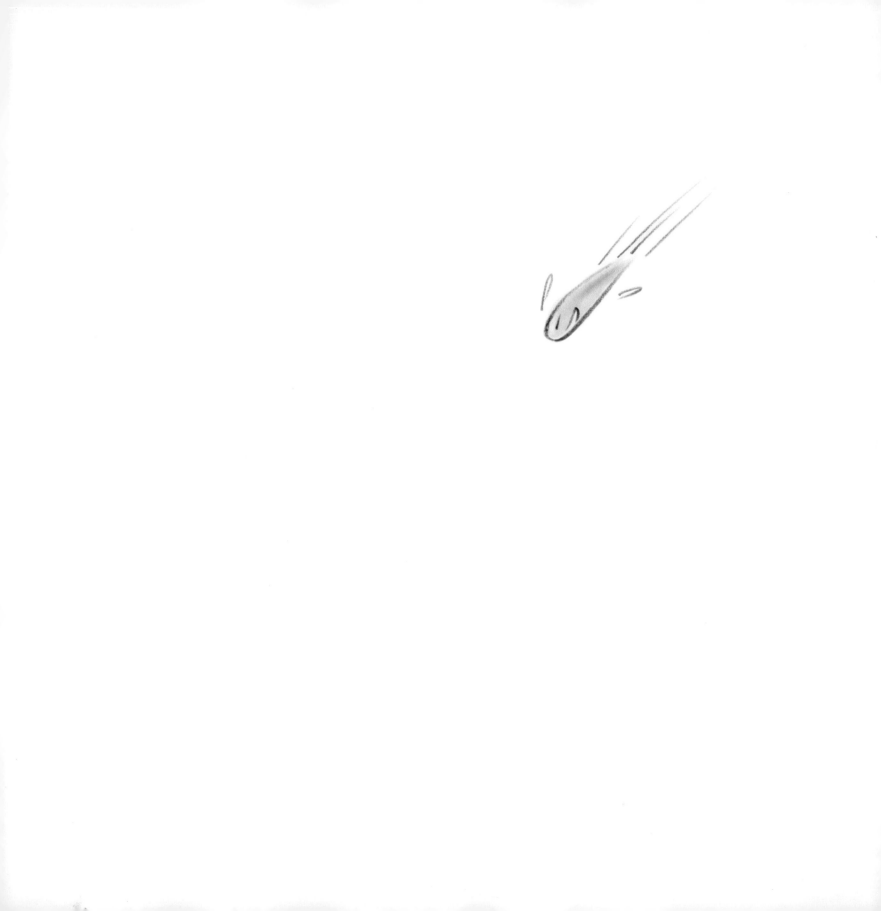

He was the happiest raindrop
in the whole wide world.

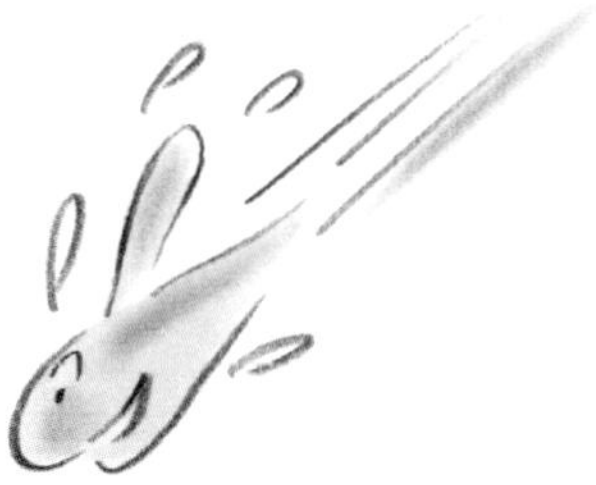

Then suddenly he had
a terrible thought—
that he was falling
instead of flying.

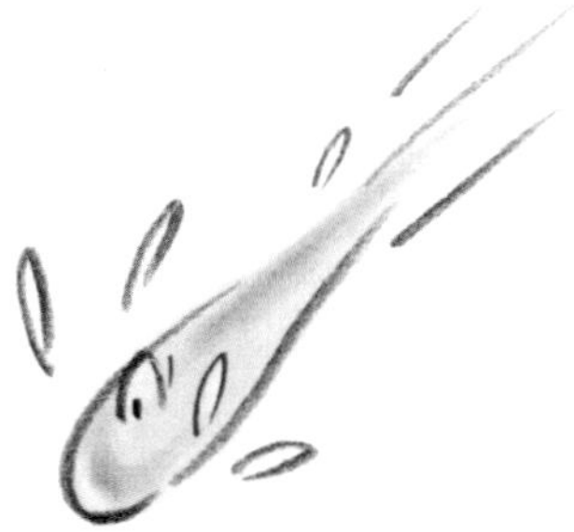

As he thought about
falling, the raindrop's
happiness vanished.

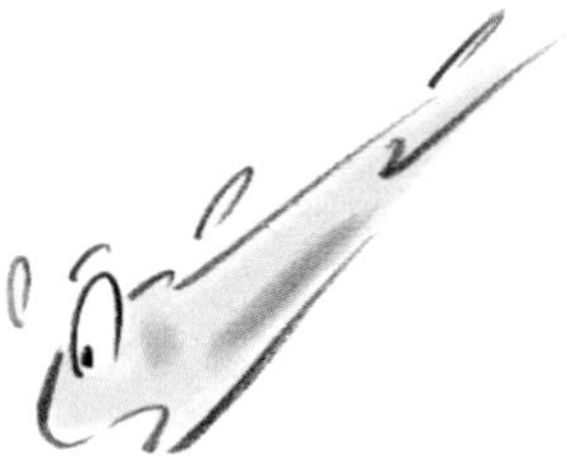

He began to worry about
crashing into a rock
             or a road
             or a field
             or a house.

And so he fell, afraid of
what might happen to him.

He missed out on the fun
of skimming through the clouds.

He missed out on the joy
of riding on the wind.

He missed out on the excitement
of racing with other raindrops.

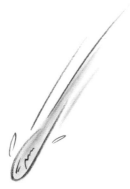

He missed out on everything.

Down, down, down he fell,
sad and scared and alone.

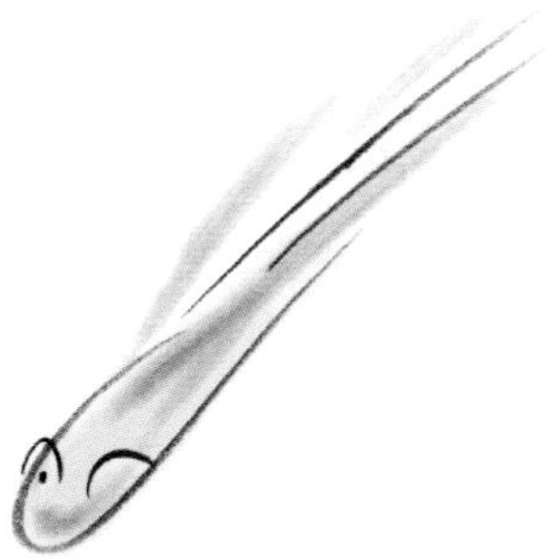

Then he saw something glowing bright on the ground far below.

It was a roaring campfire...

and the raindrop
crashed right into it.

For a few moments nothing happened.

Then a tiny cloud appeared.

The little raindrop
had become
a wisp of steam!

He had become light and airy, and, like all wisps of steam, he began rising.

And as he rose, he knew
he would join the clouds
and become a raindrop
once again.